DR JEKYLL AND MR HYDE
and
THE SUICIDE CLUB

DR JEKYLL AND MR HYDE

and

THE SUICIDE CLUB

Robert Louis Stevenson

Retold by Donald M. McFarlan

Illustrated by Dick Hart

NELSON

THOMAS NELSON AND SONS LTD
Nelson House Mayfield Road
Walton-on-Thames Surrey KT12 5PL

51 York Place
Edinburgh EH1 3JD

P.O. Box 18123
Nairobi Kenya

Yi Xiu Factory Building
Unit 05-06 5th Floor
65 Sims Avenue Singapore 1438

THOMAS NELSON (HONG KONG) LTD
Toppan Building 10/F
22A Westlands Road
Quarry Bay Hong Kong

THOMAS NELSON (NIGERIA) LTD
8 Ilupeju Bypass PMB 21303 Ikeja Lagos

ISBN 017-555207-X
NCN 740-8607-5

Printed in Hong Kong

DR JEKYLL AND MR HYDE

NOTE

Born in 1850, Robert Louis Stevenson suffered all his life from ill-health, but he never allowed this to limit his interests or to interfere with his writing.

Although he is best known for his outstanding children's story, "Treasure Island", Robert Louis Stevenson also wrote exciting novels such as "Kidnapped" and travel books of brilliant descriptive quality such as "Travels with a Donkey" and "An Inland Voyage".

The story of *Dr Jekyll and Mr Hyde* is based wholly on imagination, and was published in 1886 as a "shilling shocker"—the sort of book we call a thriller today. But it is a serious study of the struggle between good and evil that goes on in all of us, and the horrifying drama is perhaps all the more exciting because it is set against the ordinary everyday life of nineteenth century London. The comfortable households of lawyers and doctors in the days of Queen Victoria provide a striking contrast to the dark city streets outside where the violent action takes place, whether dimmed by fog or silent and deserted in the early hours of the morning. In the same way, the savagery of Edward Hyde stands out the more sharply against the kindliness of other characters in the story—and indeed of Dr Jekyll himself.

1. What lesson do you think the author was trying to teach in this story?

2. How can you tell that the story is set in the late nineteenth century and not in the middle of the twentieth century?

3. Can you find passages that show the kindly character of Mr Utterson, Dr Lanyon and Mr Poole?

4. When *Dr Jekyll and Mr Hyde* was first published "it became instantly popular". Can you suggest some reasons for this? Do you think it would be equally popular if it were published as a new book today?

1

The Story of the Door

Mr Utterson the lawyer did not often smile. His face was long and thin and sad, and his look never changed whether he was talking to good men or bad men. His friends were few, but they loved him as one of the kindest of men. One of his closest friends was Mr Richard Enfield, who was also his cousin. The two men were quite unlike one another and people who saw them used to wonder what they found to talk about on their Sunday walks together. They had not much to say to one another, and they did not smile or laugh. But each of them truly enjoyed being with his friend, and each looked forward to his weekly Sunday walk.

One day the two friends went together down a quiet street in a busy part of London. There were shops along both sides, looking as if they had been newly painted, but since it was Sunday there was no one about. Near the corner of the street on the left-hand side there was an entry to a courtyard, and just beside it a large building that looked on to the street. It showed no window on that side, nothing but a door and a plain dirty wall above. The place was very different from the nearby shops. The door had neither bell nor knocker. It was scratched and dirty and needed painting. It looked as if many years had passed since anyone had cleaned it or even opened it.

Mr Enfield and the lawyer were on the other side of the street, but when they came opposite the entry to the courtyard Mr Enfield lifted his stick and pointed.

"Did you ever notice that door?" he asked.

"Yes," said the lawyer.

"I always remember it when I come this way," Mr Enfield went on, "because of a very strange thing that happened."

The lawyer looked surprised. "What was that?"

"Well, it was this way," said Mr Enfield. "I was coming home from some place away at the other end of the town, about three o'clock on a black winter morning. My way lay through a part of the town where there was nothing to be seen but the lights in the streets. Street after street, and everyone asleep—street after street and all as empty as a church. At last I felt so lonely and afraid that I began to long for the sight of a policeman.

"All at once I saw two figures. One was a small man who was moving along at a good speed in front of me. The other was a little girl of perhaps eight or ten who was running as hard as she could down a side street. Well, sir, at the corner where the two streets met, the two of them ran into one another. Then something horrible happened. The man knocked the girl down, kicked her again and again, and left her screaming on the ground.

"I gave a shout, ran as fast as I could, and laid hold of the man. I held him fast by the collar of his coat and dragged him back to the small crowd of people who had now gathered round the screaming child. He was quite

quiet and did not try to run away, but gave me such an ugly look that I felt afraid. The people who were in the street were the little girl's own family, and soon a doctor came along. He looked her over carefully and told us that she was not badly hurt. But there was one thing everyone in the crowd thought. We hated the man who had knocked down the child, the doctor most of all. I felt sure by the way he looked at the man that he would have killed him if he could.

"We told the man that we would make him pay for this horrible act. He would have no friends in the whole of London if we told what he had done. All the time, as we spoke angrily to him, the women stood around as wild as witches. But although everyone's face was full of hate, the man in the middle was as cool as could be.

"'I do not wish to make trouble,' said he. 'What do you want me to pay?'

"We agreed that he should pay a hundred pounds to the girl's family. It was clear that he thought the sum was far too much, but he was so afraid of us that he had to say that he would pay. But where was he to get the money at that hour of the morning? We all followed him closely, and to our surprise he led us to this street and to that very door over there. He took out a key, went in, and in a short time came out again with ten pounds in gold coins and a cheque for the rest."

Mr Enfield looked at his friend.

"The name on the cheque," he said slowly, "that was the greatest surprise. I mean the man who had signed for the money. It was the name of a man well known and well liked in this town. I spoke sharply to my prisoner and told him that a man cannot walk through a dark door at four o'clock in the morning and come out of it with another man's cheque for nearly a hundred pounds. Had he stolen it?

"But my prisoner laughed at me. 'Set your mind at rest,' he said. 'I will stay with you until the bank opens, take the cheque there myself, and bring you the money.'

"So we all set off, the doctor, the child's father, the strange evil man and myself, and we spent the rest of the night in my house. I had made up my mind that I would not let him out of my sight. After breakfast we all went together to the bank. I gave in the cheque myself and said that I did not think we would get a penny for it. But I was wrong. The name written on it was in order and the money paid without question."

"A bad story," said Mr Utterson. He had been very

quiet as his friend told him all that had happened.

"Yes, it is," Mr Enfield answered. "That man was really wicked, yet the man who put his name on the cheque is the very opposite—well known for all the good things he does. What can this evil man have done to him to make him pay up for that night's wrong-doing? I do not know what made him do it, but I can never forget that house with the door."

"Do you know if the man who signed the cheque lives there?" asked Mr Utterson.

"No, he does not," said his friend. "He lives in a square somewhere in this part of the town—I forget where."

"And you never asked anyone about that house with the door?" said the lawyer.

"No, sir! I do not like asking too many questions. It often leads to trouble."

"That is very true," said the other.

"But I have had a good look at the place for myself," Mr Enfield went on. "It seems different from any other house round here. There is no other door here, and the only one who ever goes in and out of that door is the man I have been telling you about. There are three windows looking out on the courtyard, but they are always shut, though they are clean. There is a chimney and smoke comes from it, so someone must live there. Yet I am not sure, for the buildings are so close together on that side of the street that it is hard to say where one ends and the other begins."

The two men walked on again for a while without saying a word. Then Mr Utterson spoke.

"Enfield, that's a good rule of yours—I mean—not

to ask too many questions."

"Yes, I think it is," said Enfield.

"But for all that," said the lawyer, "there is one thing I must ask you. I want to know the name of that man who knocked down the child."

"Well," said Mr Enfield, "I can't see what harm it would do to tell you. It was a man named Hyde."

"What does he look like?" said Mr Utterson.

"It is not easy to tell you. I feel that there is something wrong with him, something strange and bad. I never saw a man I disliked so much, and yet I cannot tell you why. No, sir, I cannot tell you what he looks like. Yet I remember him clearly."

Again the two men walked some way without speaking. It was Mr Utterson who spoke at last.

"You are quite sure he used a key?" he asked. "To open the door, I mean."

"Yes, he did," said Mr Enfield. "Did I not tell you?"

"Of course you did," answered the other. "I know my questions must seem strange. The fact is, I know something about this already, and I also know the name of the man who signed the cheque."

"I have told you the story just as it happened," said Mr Enfield. "The man had a key, I am quite sure. He has it still. I saw him use it again, less than a week ago."

Mr Utterson said nothing to that, but he looked more troubled than ever.

"I have learned another lesson today," said the younger man, "and that is to say nothing about this strange matter. Let us not talk of Mr Hyde again."

"With all my heart!" said the lawyer. "Let us shake hands on that!"

2

The Search for Mr Hyde

That evening Mr Utterson came home with a troubled mind and sat down to eat his dinner without feeling hungry. On a Sunday evening, after this meal was over, he usually liked to sit close by the fire reading a book until the clock of a nearby church rang out the hour of twelve. Then he would go quietly to bed. But this night, as soon as he had finished eating, he took up a candle and went into his office. There he unlocked a box and took from it a large envelope. On it were written the words: "Dr Jekyll's Will". The lawyer sat down, opened the envelope, and began to read the paper that was inside.

Dr Jekyll had written his will himself, for Mr Utterson had said he would have nothing to do with it, although he was his lawyer. The paper said in a few words that if Henry Jekyll, M.D., D.C.L., LL.D., F.R.S., were to die, everything he had was to belong to his friend and helper Edward Hyde. It also said that if no one saw Dr Jekyll for three months or longer, the same man, Edward Hyde, was to have everything that had belonged to the doctor.

It was part of Mr Utterson's work as a lawyer to keep this paper safe, even if he did not like what it said. Now that he knew what a wicked man Mr Hyde was, he felt sure this piece of paper would bring trouble some day. Mr Utterson made up his mind. He got up, blew out his candle, put on a coat and set out to visit his friend, the great Dr Lanyon.

"If anyone knows what to do, it will be Dr Lanyon," he thought.

The servant at the door knew Mr Utterson and brought him right into the room where Dr Lanyon sat alone. At the sight of the lawyer he got up from his chair and held out both his hands. These two men had been friends since their days together at school. It was not long before the lawyer spoke of what was on his mind.

"I suppose, Lanyon," he said, "you and I must be the two oldest friends that Henry Jekyll has?"

"I suppose we are," said the other. "And what of that? I see little of him now."

"Is that so?" said Mr Utterson. "I thought since you are both doctors that you would often have a talk with one another."

"We did, at one time," was the answer. "But it is more than ten years since Henry Jekyll began to act very strangely. And now, although I feel friendly enough towards him because of our old days together, I see very little of him."

The next minute Dr Lanyon became very angry. "He does not act like a doctor at all," he cried. "I think he is out of his mind!"

Mr Utterson said nothing. "They have had a quarrel about something," he thought to himself. "That is what has happened." Then he asked another question. "Did you ever meet a friend of his—a man called Hyde?"

"Hyde?" said Lanyon. "No, never heard of him."

That was all the lawyer could learn from his visit, and when he reached home that night he could not get to sleep. He heard the bell of the church near his house ring six o'clock, and still he lay awake, his mind at work. As he lay in bed in the dark he thought of what Mr Enfield had told him about Hyde. He thought again of the quiet street, then of a man walking quickly, then of a child running. Then these two met and the wicked man knocked the child down and kicked her while she screamed. When he fell asleep at last, he saw the same man in his dreams, moving through the town, and at every corner he knocked down a child and left her screaming. But in the lawyer's dream the evil man had no face. That was what troubled Mr Utterson most. If only he could see the face of this man Hyde, surely he would remember him for ever.

From that time on Mr Utterson began to visit as often as he could the side street where the door was. Early in the morning before work began, in the middle of the day when there were many people in the street, at night under the light of the moon, the lawyer kept watch.

"If his name is Mr Hyde," he said to himself, "my name shall be Mr Seek!"

At last he saw what he had waited for. It was a fine dry night, frost in the air, the streets clean and empty. By ten o'clock, when the shops were shut, the side street with the door was very lonely and quiet. Mr Utterson had been watching for some time when he heard the sound of a quick light step coming near. This must be his man! Mr Utterson hid in the shadow of the entry to the courtyard and waited.

The steps came nearer and grew louder as they turned the corner of the street. The lawyer, looking out from the entry, caught sight of the man who was coming near him. He was small and had on a dark coat, and there was something very strange about him. He made straight for the door, and as he crossed the road he took a key from his pocket as if he were coming home.

Mr Utterson stepped out and touched him on the shoulder as he passed.

"Mr Hyde, I think?"

Mr Hyde jumped back as if he had been struck. But he was afraid only for a second. He did not look the lawyer in the face, but he answered easily and at once:

"That is my name. What do you want?"

"I see you are going in," answered the lawyer. "I am an old friend of Dr Jekyll's—my name is Mr Utterson. Meeting you like this, I thought you might let me into the house."

"You will not find Dr Jekyll here. He is not at home," said Mr Hyde. Then, all at once, but still without looking up, he asked: "How did you know me?"

"I want you to do something for me first," said Mr Utterson. "Will you let me see your face?"

Mr Hyde was still for a little, as if he were thinking what he should do. Then he turned quickly round, lifted his head, and the two men stared at each other for a few seconds.

"Now I shall know you again," said Mr Utterson. "It may be useful."

"Yes," said Mr Hyde. "I am glad we have met. And you had better know where my house is." He gave the lawyer the number of a house in a street in Soho.

"Good God!" thought Mr Utterson. "Can he read my mind just by looking at me? Was he also thinking about Dr Jekyll's will?" But he said nothing and only waited for Hyde to speak again.

"And now let me ask you a question," said Mr Hyde. "How did you know me?"

"Someone told me what you looked like," was the answer.

"Who was that?"

"We have friends who know us both," said Mr Utterson.

"Friends who know us both?" cried Mr Hyde. "And who are they?"

"Dr Jekyll is one," said the lawyer.

"He never told you about me," shouted Mr Hyde angrily. "I did not think you would tell me a lie."

"That is not the way to talk to me," said Mr Utterson.

The man in front of him laughed like a wild animal, then he pushed past Mr Utterson, opened the door, and went very quickly into the house.

The lawyer stood there for a little while after Mr Hyde had left him, and he looked very troubled. Then he began to move slowly along the street, stopping every step or two and putting his hand to his head like a man in pain. He could not stop thinking about the man he had just met. Mr Hyde was small and he had a very white face. He seemed to have a strange shape, almost as if he were an animal rather than a man. He had an ugly smile. He had spoken to the lawyer as if he hated him and yet at the same time as if he were afraid of him. All these things were against Hyde, but Mr Utterson was still greatly troubled.

"There must be something else," he said to himself. "There *is* something else, if only I knew what it was. The man is like an animal! Oh, my poor Harry Jekyll, if ever I saw an evil face, it is that of your new friend!"

Just round the corner from the side street there was a square of old, well-built, good-looking houses. At the door of the largest of them Mr Utterson stopped and knocked. An old servant opened the door.

"Is Dr Jekyll at home, Poole?" asked the lawyer.

"I will see, Mr Utterson," said Poole, letting the visitor into a large warm hall. "Will you wait here by the fire, sir?"

"Thank you," said the lawyer, and as he waited he

thought again of his meeting with Hyde. He could not forget the man's face, it was so evil. He was glad when Poole came back to say that his master, Dr Jekyll, had gone out.

"I saw Mr Hyde go in by the old side door, Poole," said Mr Utterson. "Is that right, when Dr Jekyll is away from home?"

"Quite right, Mr Utterson," replied the servant. "Mr Hyde has a key to the side door."

"Your master seems to like that man very much, Poole," said the lawyer.

"Yes, sir, he does. We all have orders to do whatever he tells us."

"I do not think I ever met Mr Hyde in this house," Mr Utterson went on.

"Oh no, sir. He never eats here. In fact, we see very little of him in this part of the house. He usually comes and goes by the side door."

"Well, good-night, Poole."

"Good-night, Mr Utterson."

The lawyer set out for his home with a very heavy heart.

"Poor Harry Jekyll," he thought. "I am sure he is in great trouble. This Mr Hyde must wish to do him some evil. What danger my poor friend must be in! If Hyde comes to know what is written in the will, he may do something to get Jekyll's money for himself."

Mr Utterson made up his mind. "I must do something to help, if Jekyll will only let me!"

3

Mr Utterson makes a Promise

Two weeks later, by good luck, Dr Jekyll invited a few of his oldest and best friends to dinner at his house. After the evening was over and all the others had gone home, Mr Utterson waited behind to speak to the doctor. Dr Jekyll was happy to see him stay. He sat by the fireside, a large strong man of fifty, with a bright face. You could see by his look that he was very fond of his friend Mr Utterson and was glad to have a talk with him.

"I have been wanting to speak to you, Jekyll," the lawyer began. "You know that will of yours which is in my care?"

The doctor smiled at his friend. "My poor Utterson," he said. "I never saw a man so troubled as you are by my will."

"You know that I never liked it," Utterson answered.

"Yes, I do know that," said the doctor sharply. "You have told me so, more than once."

"Well, I tell you so again," the lawyer went on. "I have been hearing something of young Hyde."

The large good-looking face of Dr Jekyll grew white even to his lips, and he spoke angrily. "I do not wish to hear any more," he said. "This is something I thought we had said we would never talk about."

"What I heard about Hyde was very bad," said Utterson.

"It cannot make me change my will. You do not understand—no, you do not!" The doctor was plainly troubled. "I cannot tell you about it, so it is no good speaking of the matter any more."

"Jekyll," said Utterson. "You know me. I am a man of my word. I am your friend as well as your lawyer. Tell me now what is troubling you, and I have no doubt I can help you."

"My dear Utterson," said the doctor, "this is very good of you, yes, very good of you, and I cannot find words to thank you enough. I believe you and I would try to please you before any man alive, before myself, if I were free to choose. But, in fact, things are not as bad as you think. And just to put your good heart at rest, I will tell you one thing. The minute I choose, I can be free of Mr Hyde. I give you my hand on that, and I thank you again.

"I will add just one thing more, Utterson," the doctor went on. "This is my own trouble, and I beg you to leave it alone."

Utterson was quiet for a little, looking into the fire.

"I have no doubt you are quite right," he said at last, as he got to his feet to go home.

"Well, since we have talked about this for the last time, I hope," said the doctor, "there is one thing I should like you to know. I have really a very great interest in poor Hyde. I know you have seen him; he told me so; and I'm afraid he was rude to you. But I do take a great interest in that young man, and if anything happens to me, Utterson, I want you to be sure to help him. I think you would do it, if you knew all that I could tell you. Please give me your word, for my sake."

"You know that I shall never like him," said the lawyer.

"I don't ask that," said Jekyll, laying his hand on the other's arm. "I only ask you to be just. I only ask you to help him for my sake, when I am no longer here."

Utterson gave a deep sigh. "Very well," he said. "I give you my word."

And with that he made his way home.

4

The Murder in the Lane

Nearly a year later, the news of a horrible crime spread through the town of London. A young girl who was a servant in a house not far from the river had gone upstairs to bed about eleven o'clock. The sky was quite clear during the early part of the night, and the lane which the girl could see from her window was brightly lit by a full moon. She was alone in the house, and before she went to bed she sat by the window looking out.

As she sat there, she saw an old gentleman with white hair coming along the lane near the house. A minute or two later she saw another man, younger and much smaller, coming the other way, as if he wished to meet the old gentleman. They met just outside the house, so that the girl was able to see the older man stopping to speak to the other. He pointed with his hand as if he were asking the way. The moon shone on his face as he spoke and the girl thought what a kind and pleasant old gentleman he looked. The next minute she saw who the other man was. It was a Mr Hyde who had once visited her own master, and whom she did not like at all.

Mr Hyde had a heavy stick in his hand. He did not answer a word when the old gentleman spoke to him. It was almost as if he were angry at being stopped at all. He let out a great cry of anger, stamped his foot, shook his stick, and jumped about like a wild animal.

The old gentleman took a step back as if he were very surprised. At that Mr Hyde lifted his hand and knocked him to the ground with his stick. The next instant he was kicking the old man under foot and hitting him with the stick again and again. It was so horrible the girl fainted.

It was two o'clock in the morning before she came to herself and was able to call the police. The murderer had gone long ago, but the body still lay in the middle of the lane, cut and blood-stained all over. The stick which had been used, although it was of very hard and heavy wood, had broken in the middle. One half had rolled to the side of the road, the other, no doubt, had been carried away by the murderer. A purse and a gold watch were found on the victim, but except for a letter which he had been carrying to the post, there were no papers to tell who he was. The letter had the name and address of Mr Utterson on it.

The letter was brought to the lawyer the next morning before he was out of bed. When he looked at it and heard where it had been found he said: "I shall say nothing till I have seen the body. This will bring a lot of trouble. Please wait here until I am dressed and ready." He hurried through his breakfast as quickly as he could and then went to the police station to which the body of the old gentleman had been carried. As soon as he came into the room where it lay, Mr Utterson spoke.

"Yes," said he, "I know him. I am sorry to say that this is Sir Danvers Carew."

"Good God, sir," said the police officer. "Is it possible? This is a very bad thing to have happened. Perhaps you can also help us to find the man who killed him." Then he quickly told what the girl had seen, and showed the lawyer the broken stick.

Mr Utterson shook his head when he heard the name of Hyde, but when the stick was laid before him he was quite sure. Broken and useless though it now was, he remembered it. He had given that very stick as a present to Henry Jekyll many years before.

"Is this Mr Hyde a small man?" he asked.

"Very small and very evil-looking, so the maid told us," said the officer.

Mr Utterson thought for a moment, then he looked at the policeman.

"If you will come with me in my cab, I think I can take you to his house."

By this time it was about nine in the morning, and the first fog of the year had spread over the town. The lawyer's thoughts were as dark as the sky, and when he looked at the policeman he was filled with fright at what might happen.

As the cab drew up in front of the house to which Mr Utterson had brought them, the fog lifted a little. The lawyer could see a dirty street with some poor shops where many ragged children stood watching them from the doorways. Just then the fog came down again, dark and brown, so that he could not even see the house at which they had stopped. This was the home of Henry Jekyll's friend—heir to a quarter of a million pounds.

A woman with a white face and silver hair opened the door to them. She had an evil look, but she spoke quite politely. Yes, she told them, this was Mr Hyde's house, but he was not at home. He had been in that night very late, but had gone away again in less than an hour. There was nothing strange about that. He was often away from home. For instance, till yesterday it had been nearly two months since she had seen him.

"Very well then, we wish to see his rooms," said the lawyer. When the woman said that they could not do so, he added: "I had better tell you who this is. It is Inspector Newcomen of Scotland Yard."

A flash of evil joy appeared on the woman's face.

"Ah," she said, "he is in trouble! What has he done?"

Mr Utterson and the police officer looked at one another.

"He doesn't seem a much-liked man," said the policeman. "And now, my good woman, just let me and this gentleman have a look around."

In the whole of the house Mr Hyde used only two of the rooms, but these looked like the home of a very rich man. There were bottles of wine in the cupboard; the knives, forks, and spoons for the table were silver; a good picture hung on the wall; and the carpets were thick and of fine colour. As the two men went in, however, the rooms looked as if they had been turned upside down. Clothes lay about the floor with their pockets turned inside out. Drawers stood wide open. In the fireplace there lay a pile of grey ashes, as if some papers had been burned in a great hurry.

The inspector bent down to have a closer look at the ashes. He pulled out the end of a cheque-book which had not been burned right through. Then he found the other half of the broken stick behind the door. The police officer was very pleased. He was sure he knew enough now to catch the murderer. Then Mr Utterson and he visited the bank, where they found that Mr Hyde had several thousand pounds.

"You may be sure of it, sir," the inspector said to Mr Utterson, "I have him in my hand now. He must have lost his head or he would never have left the stick in that room or burned the cheque-book. Why, money is life to the man. We have nothing to do but wait for him at the bank and catch him when he comes there."

But this was not so easy. Mr Hyde seemed to have very few friends. No one knew anything about his family. He had never been photographed. The few people who had seen him were not even able to say very well what he looked like. But one thing they all said : his body was twisted, more like an animal than a man.

5

The Writing in the Letter

It was late in the afternoon when Mr Utterson made his way to Dr Jekyll's house. Poole, the doctor's servant, opened the door to him at once, and took him through the house and across a courtyard which at one time had been a garden. They came to a dark, ugly building which stood on its own at the end of the courtyard. There were no windows on that side. Mr Utterson looked around the dusty place with interest. It was plain that the building had not been used for many years.

At the far end there were stairs leading up to a closed door. Mr Utterson went up and through the door into Dr Jekyll's study. It was a large room with plenty of furniture—chairs and a table, cupboards round each wall, and a long mirror standing on the floor. The dusty windows which looked out on to the courtyard had iron bars on them. The fire was burning brightly and a lamp was already lit because the fog had made everything dark that day. There, close to the warm fire, sat Dr Jekyll, looking very sick. He did not rise but held out a cold hand and spoke in a weak voice.

"And now," said Mr Utterson, as soon as Poole had left them, "I expect you have heard the news?"

The doctor was as white as a ghost. "They were shouting it in the street," he said. "I heard them."

"I must ask you one question at once," said the lawyer. "I was Carew's lawyer, but I am yours also, and I want to know what I am doing. You have not been silly enough to have this man Hyde in your house?"

"Utterson, I give you my word," cried the doctor, "I give you my word I will never set eyes on him again. And I give you my word that I am done with him for ever. It is all at an end. In fact, he does not want my help now. You do not know him as I do. He is safe, he is quite safe. Believe me, he will not be heard of any more."

The lawyer listened sadly. He did not like to see his friend looking so ill and troubled.

"You seem very sure of him," he said, "and, for your sake, I hope you are right. If the man were caught and brought to court, he might give away your name."

"I am quite sure of him," said Jekyll again. "I cannot tell you why—it is a secret. But there is one way you may help me. I have—I have had a letter, and I don't know whether to show it to the police or not. I should like to leave it in your hands, Utterson. You will know what to do, I am sure."

"I suppose you are afraid that the letter might help the police to catch him?" asked the lawyer.

"No," said the other, "I don't care what happens to Hyde. I am done with him for ever. No, I was thinking of my own good name. You see, I am now mixed up with this horrible murder. People will talk about me. They know that I have been a friend of Hyde's."

Utterson thought for a while. He was surprised to find how easily his friend wished to get rid of Hyde.

"Well," he said at last, "let me see the letter."

The letter was written in a strange way, and the

name at the bottom of it was "Edward Hyde". It said that Dr Jekyll was not to trouble at all about the writer, as he was sure to get away. He was sorry that he had been so much trouble to the good doctor who had helped him a thousand times over.

The lawyer was quite pleased with the letter. Perhaps Dr Jekyll had been too kind to the evil Hyde, but that was all. Mr Utterson was angry with himself for some of his past unkind thoughts.

"Have you the envelope?" he asked. "Where did it come from?"

"I burned the envelope," answered Jekyll, "before I thought what I was doing. But it had no postmark. The letter was brought by hand to the house."

"Shall I keep this and think what to do about it?" asked Utterson.

"I want you to do what you think best," was the answer. "I am not well. I cannot act by myself now."

"Well, I shall think about it," said the lawyer. "Now, just one more question. Was it Hyde who made you write your will, leaving everything you have to him? Did he tell you what to write?"

The doctor became whiter in the face than ever. He shut his mouth tight and said nothing.

"I knew it," said Utterson. "He meant to murder you too, for money. You have had a lucky escape."

"I have had something far better," said the doctor. "I have had a lesson. O God, Utterson, what a lesson I have had!" He covered his face with his hands. He had no more to say.

On his way out, the lawyer stopped and had a word or two with Poole.

"There was a letter handed in today," he said. "Can you tell me who brought it? What did he look like?"

Poole shook his head. "No letter has come here today, except by the post," he said. "I am quite sure that no letter was handed in."

This news sent the visitor away with all his troubles alive once again. It was clear that the letter must have come to the door of the doctor's study, not to the front door of his house. Perhaps it had even been written in the study. Had Dr Jekyll told him the truth? Where was Mr Hyde?

The newspapers were full of the story of the death of Sir Danvers Carew. "Shocking murder of an M.P." What was Mr Utterson to do about the letter? One of his friends was dead. The good name of another was in danger. The lawyer made up his mind to talk the whole thing over with his clerk. Perhaps he could help him.

A little later he sat on one side of the fire in his own house, with Mr Guest, his head clerk, on the other. Mr Utterson brought out a bottle of wine for them to drink as they talked. There was still a lot of fog in the town outside, but the room was warm and well lit.

For once the lawyer smiled. Mr Guest was a man he liked and could talk to as a friend. He kept no secrets from him. Guest knew the people they were going to talk about. He had often been at the doctor's house; he knew Poole; he must have heard about Mr Hyde.

"This is sad news about Sir Danvers Carew," Mr Utterson began.

"Yes, sir, it is," said Guest. "Many people have been talking about it. The man who did this horrible thing must have been out of his mind."

"I should like to hear what you have to say about that," said Mr Utterson. "I have a letter here which he is said to have written. I don't want you to talk about it to anyone else. But there it is, look at it."

Guest took the letter and sat down at once to read it carefully. "No, sir," he said in a little while. "Not out of his mind; but it is strange writing."

"And a very strange writer, from all I hear," said Mr Utterson.

Just then the servant came in with a letter.

"Is that from Dr Jekyll, sir?" asked the clerk. "I thought I knew the writing. May I see it?"

"It is only a short note asking me to come to dinner with him," said the lawyer. "Why do you want to see it?"

"One moment. Thank you, sir." The clerk took the two letters and put them side by side on the table. He looked at them both closely before he gave them back.

"Thank you, sir," he said at last. "Very interesting writing."

Mr Utterson was quiet. Then all at once he spoke.

"Why did you put the two letters side by side, Guest?" he asked.

"Well, sir," replied the clerk, "they look very like one another. Not quite the same, and yet I think one man wrote them both. Very strange, indeed."

"You will not tell anyone about this," said the lawyer.

"No, sir," said the clerk. "I shall keep quiet."

When Mr Utterson was alone once more, he locked the note in a strong-box.

"My God!" he said to himself. "My friend Henry Jekyll has written this letter for a murderer!"

6

A Visit to Dr Lanyon

Thousands of pounds were to be given to anyone who could catch the murderer, for Sir Danvers Carew had been a well-known and well-liked man in London. But there was no sign of Mr Hyde. The police were able to find out a good deal about him and his wicked crimes in the past. They knew that he was a very bad man. But no one could find him now. From the time he had left his house on the morning of the murder, he was lost to sight.

As time went on, Mr Utterson began to think that all was well. True, Sir Danvers was dead, and that was sad and horrible. But perhaps some good had come from it —Mr Hyde was gone. Now that Hyde was no longer to be seen, a new life began for Dr Jekyll. He came out of his house again, met his friends, and was as busy as ever. His face showed how happy he was, he did good, and for more than two months the doctor was at peace.

On the 8th of January Mr Utterson had dined at the doctor's house with a small party of his friends. Dr Lanyon had been there also, and Henry Jekyll had been very pleased to see both men. It was like the old days when the three of them were the best of friends. But on the 12th of January, and again on the 14th, the door was shut against the lawyer.

2

"Yes, the doctor is in the house," said Poole, "but he does not wish to see anyone."

On the 15th of January Mr Utterson tried again, but could not get in. This was very strange. For the past two months he had seen his friend almost every day. Why did the doctor shut him out now? Mr Utterson was very troubled once again and he made up his mind to go and see Dr Lanyon.

At that house he was shown in at once, but when he met Dr Lanyon he was frightened at the sight of his face. The man had grown white; he was as thin as a pole; he looked old and very ill. Worst of all, he seemed to be very afraid of something. What could it be?

When Utterson asked him what was wrong, the doctor answered at once.

"I have had a great fright," he said, "and I shall never be well again. I shall die in a few weeks. Well, life has been good. I liked it. Yes, sir, I used to like it. But I am near the end."

"Jekyll is ill, too," said Utterson. "Have you seen him?"

Lanyon's face changed at once and he held up a hand.

"I wish to hear or see no more of Dr Jekyll," he said in a loud voice. "I am done with him for ever. I ask you not to speak of him. He is as good as dead to me."

"No, no, do not talk like that," said Mr Utterson. Then, after a time he asked: "Can't I do anything? We are three very old friends, Lanyon."

"Nothing can be done," said Lanyon. "Ask Jekyll himself."

"He will not see me," said the lawyer.

"I am not surprised at that," was the answer. "Some

day, Utterson, after I am dead, you may perhaps come to know all that has happened. I cannot tell you just now. Never say that man's name to me again."

As soon as he got home, Mr Utterson sat down and wrote a letter to Jekyll, asking why he would not let him into his house and also why there was trouble between him and Lanyon. The next day an answer came from the doctor.

"I do not blame our old friend Lanyon," wrote Jekyll, "but it is a fact that we must never meet again. I am going to shut myself up in my house now and see no one. Even you, my old friend, will not be shown in. I am in great danger, and there is no one to blame but myself. But I am in great trouble, too, my dear Utterson. The one thing you can do to help me is to say nothing about me to anyone."

What was Utterson to do? Hyde had gone, and the doctor had seemed as happy as ever again. A week ago all was well. Now he had lost his two best friends and his thoughts were dark again. What was wrong? Had Dr Jekyll gone out of his mind?

A week later Dr Lanyon was ill in bed, and in less than a fortnight he was dead. A day or two after Lanyon's death Mr Utterson went into his office and took from his strong-box an envelope with his dead friend's writing on it:

"SECRET : for the hands of J. G. Utterson ALONE."

He opened the envelope. Inside was another envelope, carefully sealed. On the outside was written : "Not to be opened till the death of Dr Henry Jekyll." It also said that Jekyll might go away altogether. Utterson could hardly believe his eyes. The envelope had almost the same words as Henry Jekyll's own will. But why should Dr Jekyll go away for ever? In the doctor's will Mr Hyde's name was written, but he was gone now. What was it that Lanyon had written in this last letter of his? Mr Utterson wanted very much to know, but he could not open the letter—not yet.

Once again Utterson tried to see Dr Jekyll, but as usual he got no farther than the front door of the house. Poole could only tell him that his master never left his study. Sometimes he even slept there. Day after day he was there alone. He had grown very quiet, he did not read much, he seemed to have some great trouble on his mind. Utterson could only go away with that sad news. What would happen now?

7

Dr Jekyll Speaks

On the next Sunday Mr Utterson was on his usual walk with his young friend Mr Enfield. They went once again along the side street with the well-known door in it. When they came to the door they both stopped.

"Well," said Enfield, "that story is at an end. We shall never see Mr Hyde again."

"I hope not," said Utterson. "Did I ever tell you that I once met him? An evil man, if ever there was one."

"Indeed he was," said Enfield. "And, by the way, I found out something else. This door is a back way into Dr Jekyll's own house."

"So you found that out, did you?" said Utterson. "To tell you the truth, I am very troubled about poor Jekyll. Even out in the courtyard here I feel as if a friend might do him some good just by being near him, even if I am shut out of his home."

The courtyard was cold and rather dark. As they stood there, the two men saw that the middle one of the three barred windows was half-open. Sitting close beside it, like a prisoner in his cell, Utterson saw Dr Jekyll.

"Hello, Jekyll!" he cried. "I hope you are better?"

"I am very ill, Utterson," said the doctor sadly, "very ill. It will not last long now, thank God."

"You stay too much in the house," said the lawyer.

"You should be out taking a walk, like Mr Enfield and me. Come now, get your hat and come for a walk."

"You are very kind," said the other. "I should like to very much. But no, no, no! It is no good. I cannot do it. But my dear Utterson, I am very glad to see you. This is a great pleasure. I would ask you and Mr Enfield to come in, but my study is really not tidy enough."

"Why then," said the lawyer, "the best thing we can do is to stay and speak with you from where we are."

"That was just what I was going to say," answered the doctor with a smile. But no sooner had he spoken than the smile went from his face. All at once he looked the most frightened man on earth. The two friends saw it only for an instant, for the window was shut at once. But that one look was enough—Dr Jekyll was in great fear of something or someone.

The two men turned and left the courtyard without a word. They walked together along the street. At last Mr Utterson turned and looked at his friend.

"God help us!" he said. "God help us!"

But Mr Enfield was too troubled to speak at all. He just looked sadly back at Mr Utterson and walked on.

One evening some time after this meeting, Mr Utterson had a visit from Poole, Dr Jekyll's man-servant.

"Bless me, Poole, what brings you here?" he cried. Then, taking a second look at the man's face, he added:

"What is wrong? Is the doctor ill?"

"Mr Utterson," said the man, "there is something very wrong."

"Take a seat, and here is a glass of wine for you," said the lawyer. "Now, take your time and tell me why you have come."

"You know the doctor's ways, sir," said Poole, "and how he shuts himself up in his room. Well, he's shut up again in his study, and I don't like it, sir—I don't like it at all. Mr Utterson, sir, I'm afraid."

"Now, my good man," said the lawyer, "tell me at once. What are you afraid of?"

"I've been afraid for about a week," Poole went on, as if he had not heard the question, "and I can't bear it any more."

The man was plainly in great trouble. He did not look the lawyer in the face. Even now he sat with the glass of wine on his knee, staring down at the floor.

"I can't bear it any more," he said again.

"Come now," said the lawyer, "I see you have some good cause for coming to see me, Poole. I see there must be something wrong. Try to tell me what it is."

"I think there's been foul play," said Poole in a whisper.

"Foul play!" said the lawyer. "What foul play? What in the world do you mean?"

"I cannot tell you, sir," was the answer. "But will you come along with me and see for yourself?"

Mr Utterson rose at once, put on his hat and coat, and the two men went out together. It was a wild, cold, windy night in March, with a half-moon in the sky. The wind made talking difficult as they went along, and it seemed to have swept everyone else from the streets, they were so empty. The square, when they came to it, was full of wind and dust and the small trees in the garden were moving to and fro in the storm.

Poole stopped when they came to the house, his face white with fear.

"Well, sir," he said, "here we are, and please God there be nothing wrong."

"Amen, Poole," said the lawyer.

The servant knocked quietly on the door and almost at once a voice spoke from inside : "Is that you, Poole ?"

"It's all right," said Poole. "Open the door."

The hall, when they went in, was well lit; there was a big fire burning, and all the servants of the house, men and women, stood close together like sheep. At the sight of Mr Utterson one of the girls began to cry, and the cook cried out : "Bless God! It's Mr Utterson."

"What are you all doing here?" asked the lawyer. "It's not right. Your master would not be pleased."

"They're all afraid," said Poole.

They were all quiet at that, waiting to see what was going to happen.

"Now," said Poole to a boy who stood near, "give me a candle and we'll go at once."

He asked Mr Utterson to follow him, and led the way to the garden at the back of the house.

"Now, sir," said he, "you come as quietly as you can. I want you to hear, but I don't want you to be heard. And see here, sir, if by any chance he asks you to go into his room, don't go!"

Mr Utterson started at these words. What did Poole mean? Then he followed the servant into the dark building at the end of the courtyard until he came to the foot of the stairs. Here Poole signed to him to stand still and listen. He himself put down the candle and went bravely up the steps to knock on the door of the study.

"Mr Utterson, sir, asking to see you," he called. As he did so, he once again signed to the lawyer to listen.

A voice answered from inside the room. "Tell him I cannot see anyone."

"Thank you, sir," said Poole, and taking up his candle he led Mr Utterson back across the courtyard and into the big kitchen.

"Sir," he said, looking Mr Utterson in the eyes, "was that my master's voice?"

"It did not sound like it," said the lawyer, looking straight back at him. "It seems much changed."

"Changed? Yes, I think so," said the servant. "Have I been twenty years in this man's house and not know his voice? No, sir! My master has been murdered! He was murdered eight days ago when we heard him cry out. And who is there instead of him, and why the man stays there, God alone knows, Mr Utterson!"

8

The Last Night

"This is a very strange story you have to tell, Poole," said Mr Utterson. "A very wild one, my man. Suppose it were true—if Dr Jekyll has been murdered—why should the murderer stay there in his room?"

"Well, Mr Utterson," said Poole, "all I can tell you is this. All this last week he, or whatever it is that lives in that study, has been crying out night and day for some sort of medicine. My master sometimes used to write his orders to me on a piece of paper and leave it on the stair. Well, we've had nothing else for a week now. Papers on the stair every day, and a closed door so that we can't see who leaves them there. Even his food is to be left outside the door and taken in when no one is looking. Well, sir, every day, yes, two and three times a day, I have had papers sending me all over the town for the medicine he needs. Every time I brought the stuff back, there would be another paper telling me to take it away again. It was not the right medicine, or not pure enough. I had to try again."

"Have you any of these papers?" asked Mr Utterson.

Poole felt in his pocket and brought out a note which the lawyer took near the candle so that he could see to read it. The paper said:

"Dr Jekyll sends his orders to Messrs Maw the

Chemists. He wishes them to know that their last lot of medicine is not pure and is quite useless to him. A few years ago Dr Jekyll bought a large amount from Messrs Maw. He now asks them to look carefully and send that same kind of medicine to him at once. It is very important."

The letter ended in a very different way, like a man crying out for help:

"For God's sake," it said, "find me some of the old medicine!"

"This is a strange note," said Mr Utterson. "Why have you got it now?"

"The man at Maw the Chemists was so angry, sir, he threw it back at me," said Poole.

"You are sure that this is the doctor's writing?" asked the lawyer.

"I thought it looked like it," said the servant. "But what does that matter? I've seen him!"

"Seen him?" said Mr Utterson. "When and where?"

"It was this way," answered Poole. "I came quietly into the building from the courtyard. It seems he had come out to look for this medicine, or whatever it is, for the study door was open. He looked up when I came in, gave a kind of cry, and ran upstairs into the study. I saw him only for a minute, but I had the fright of my life. Sir, if that was my master, why had he a mask on his face? If it was my master, why did he cry out like a wild animal and run away from me? I have served him long enough."

"These are all very strange things," said Mr Utterson. "But I think I know what has happened. Your master, Poole, has some illness that changes his voice and his looks. That must be why he wears a mask. That is why he needs to find the right medicine. He is a doctor —he knows what will make him well again."

"Sir," said the servant, "that thing was not my master, and there's the truth. My master is a tall, fine-looking man. This thing was small, more like an animal than a man."

"No, no," said Utterson. "Don't say that."

"Oh, sir," cried Poole, "do you think I do not know my master after twenty years? No, sir, that thing in the mask was never Dr Jekyll. God knows what it was, but it was never Dr Jekyll. I am quite sure my master has been murdered."

"Poole," said the lawyer, "if you say that again, I must go and make sure. No matter what Dr Jekyll has said about not wanting to see me, I must go and break down that door."

"Ah, Mr Utterson, that's the way to talk," cried the servant. "I knew you would know what to do."

"Well now, who is to do it?" Utterson went on.

"Why, you and me, sir," was the answer. "There is an axe in that building for me, and you can carry the kitchen poker for yourself."

The lawyer took up the poker and shook it.

"Do you know, Poole," he said, "I think you and I are going to put ourselves in some danger."

"Yes, sir, that is very true," replied the servant.

"Well, then, we should speak plainly before we go," said Mr Utterson. "That thing with the mask on its face —did you know who it was?"

"Well, sir, it went so quick, and the thing was bent down nearly to the ground—I'm not quite sure. But if you mean, was it Mr Hyde?—why, yes, I think it was! You see, it was about his size, and it had the same quick way of moving. Who else could have got in by the door in the side street? He still had the key, I know that. But that's not all. I don't know, Mr Utterson, if you ever met this Mr Hyde?"

"Yes," said the lawyer, "I once spoke to him."

"Then you must know, as well as the rest of us, that there was something queer about that man—something wicked, I mean."

"I know what you are trying to say," answered Mr Utterson. "I have felt it, too."

"Yes, sir," said Poole. "Well, when that masked thing jumped like a monkey and ran up the stairs, I felt it, like something cold in the air, cold and wicked. I am quite sure that it was Mr Hyde."

"I'm afraid you are right," said the lawyer. "Yes, I believe you. I think poor Henry Jekyll is killed and I believe his murderer is still in that room there. Well, let us go and find out at once. Call Bradshaw."

Another servant came at the call, very white and frightened.

"Get ready, Bradshaw," said the lawyer. "Poole and I are going to break our way into the study. If all is well I shall take the blame. But if there is really anything wrong, or if anyone tries to get away by the other door, we must stop him. You and the boy must take sticks in your hands and go round to the door in the side street. We will give you ten minutes to get there and be ready."

As Bradshaw left, the lawyer looked at his watch.

"Now, Poole, let us go," he said; and, taking the poker under his arm, he led the way into the courtyard.

A cloud had covered the moon and it was now quite dark. The wind blew the flame of the candle to and fro as they moved near the building at the end of the court-yard. They sat down to wait. Near at hand they could hear the sound of steps moving up and down on the floor of the study above their heads.

"So it will walk all day, sir," whispered Poole, "yes, and most of the night, too. It is a wicked sound. But listen again, Mr Utterson. Tell me, is that the doctor's step?"

The steps were light and quick. The sound was quite different from the heavy step of Henry Jekyll.

"Has there never been anything else?" said Utterson.

Poole answered. "Once," he said. "Once I heard it crying."

"Crying? In what way?" said the lawyer.

"Crying like a woman or a lost child," said the servant. "I could not forget it."

But now the ten minutes were at an end. Poole found the axe. The candle was put down on a table to give them light. They drew near to the door of the study where the steps were still going up and down, up and down in the quiet of the night.

"Jekyll," cried Utterson with a loud voice, "I want to see you." He waited for a second, but no answer came. "I tell you, I must and shall see you. If you will not open, then I shall break down the door."

"Utterson," said a voice from inside, "for God's sake, go away!"

"Ah, that's not Jekyll's voice, it's Hyde's!" cried Utterson. "Down with the door, Poole!"

Poole swung the axe over his shoulder. The blow

shook the building and the door cracked under the axe. A wild cry, like that of a frightened animal, came from the study.

Up went the axe again and again. Four times the blow fell, but the wood was strong. It was not until the fifth blow that the lock broke and the door fell in on the carpet.

The two men stood back for an instant and looked into the room. All was quiet now. There was the study before their eyes in the soft lamplight. A good fire was burning; there were papers on the table, and dishes were set out for tea. It seemed the quietest room in the whole of London. Surely there was nothing wrong here?

Right in the middle of the floor lay the body of a man face down, twisted in a strange shape. They went in

quietly, turned it on its back, and looked down on the
face of Edward Hyde. He was dressed in clothes far too
big for him, clothes the size of the doctor's. His face still
seemed to move a little, but life was gone. In his hand
was a glass of poison which he had taken only a second
or two before. Utterson knew that he was looking on the
body of a man who had taken his own life.

"We have come too late," he said. "Hyde is dead.
The only thing for us to do now is to find the body of
your master."

The building was large, and, except for the study, it
was very dark. The two men hunted everywhere, from
the roof to the ground-floor, room by room, cupboard by
cupboard. Nowhere was there any sign of Henry Jekyll,
dead or alive. Poole walked up and down the stone floor
that led out to the courtyard.

"He must be buried here," he said.

"Or he may have run away," answered Utterson, and
he turned to have a look at the door that led to the side
street. It was locked, and lying on the floor near it they
found the key.

"It has not been used for some time, by the look of it,"
said the lawyer.

"Used?" cried Poole. "Do you not see, sir, it is
broken? There is no way to open the door."

"I don't know what this means," said the lawyer.
"Let us go back to the study."

They went up the stairs together and began to hunt
all through the study. On one table there were little
heaps of what looked like salt.

"That is the medicine I was always bringing him,"
said Poole.

A soft chair stood near the fire. A cup of tea had been poured out. A book lay open as if someone had sat there reading quietly by the fireside. But there was no one there, except the body on the floor. As they moved round the room the two men came to the long mirror that stood on the floor. As they looked in it they saw only the firelight and their own white and frightened faces.

"This mirror has seen some strange things, sir," whispered Poole.

"But what could Jekyll want with it?" said the lawyer.

"You may ask that!" answered Poole. "What did he want with it?"

Next they turned to the table with the papers on it. Among them was a large envelope with the name of Mr Utterson on it, written by the doctor himself. The lawyer opened it, and several papers fell to the ground. The first was a will, in much the same words as the one which the lawyer had in the box in his office. It said what was to be done if Dr Jekyll died or went away from his home. But this time, in place of the name Edward Hyde, the lawyer read his own name: Gabriel John Utterson. He looked at Poole, then back at the paper in his hand, and last of all at the dead man on the floor.

"My head goes round," he said. "I do not know what to think. The money and everything else was to be his. Yet he did not burn this new will which took it all away from him."

He took up the next paper and read it. It was very short, also written by the doctor, and with that day's date at the top.

"Oh, Poole!" Mr Utterson cried out, "he was alive

and here this day! He must still be alive. He must have run away. But why, and how? We must be careful, you and I. We must be sure we do not blame your master for killing this man."

"Why don't you read the paper, sir?" asked Poole.

"Because I am afraid," replied the lawyer. "God help me, I hope there is nothing wrong here!"

He lifted the paper and read:

"MY DEAR UTTERSON,

When this shall come into your hands I shall have gone away for ever. I am sure that the end is coming soon, very soon. Go, then, and first of all read the letter which Lanyon said he was going to give you. Then, if you wish to know more, read the other papers which you will find with this.

Your unhappy friend,

HENRY JEKYLL."

"Here are the other papers," said Poole. He gave the lawyer a fat envelope which was still sealed. The lawyer put it in his pocket.

"I will say nothing about this just now," he said. "If your master has run away or is dead we will keep it quiet. It is now ten o'clock. I must go home and read all these papers by myself, but I shall be back before midnight. Then we shall send for the police."

They went out, locking the door of the dark building behind them. Mr Utterson left the servants gathered round the fire in the hall once more. He walked slowly back to his office to read the two long letters in which the whole story was made clear.

9

Dr Lanyon's Letter

Mr Utterson took from his box the letter in Dr Lanyon's writing which said: "Not to be opened till the death of Dr Henry Jekyll." Jekyll was nowhere to be found, alive or dead. The lawyer knew that he must open this letter at once, to find out if he could what had happened. This is what he read, the story Dr Lanyon had to tell:

On the ninth of January a letter came to me from my old friend Henry Jekyll. I was surprised by this, because we did not usually write to one another. I had seen the doctor only the night before, and had dinner with him. I was even more surprised when I read the letter:

10th December, 18—

"DEAR LANYON,

You are one of my oldest friends, and you have always been good to me. Lanyon, I need your help, this very night. It is a matter of life and death. I want you to leave anything else you are doing tonight, no matter what it is. Take a cab, bring this letter with you to let you know what to do, and come straight to my house.

Poole, my man-servant, knows what to do. You will find him waiting for you, and a locksmith with him. The door of my study is to be opened by force and you are to go in alone. Then you must go straight to the cupboard with the glass door which you will see on your left hand. If it is shut, break the lock. Take out the fourth drawer from the top. You will find that it has in it some powders, a bottle, and a small notebook. I beg you to carry away the drawer with these things in it to your house at once.

That is the first thing I want you to do. Now for the second. You should be back, if you set out as soon as you get this letter, long before midnight. I hope your servants will all be in bed before twelve o'clock because what you have to do is secret. At midnight, then, I want you to be alone in your room. A man will come to your house, and you are to open the door to him yourself. He will tell you that he comes from me, and you are to give him the drawer which you have brought from my study. That is all you have to do—and my thanks will always be with you. My dear friend, you must do this for me. If not you may drive me mad, or even cause my death.

I am sure you will help me. If not, you will know that you have seen the last of Henry Jekyll. I am in great trouble. Do this for me, my dear Lanyon, and save

Your friend,

H.J."

When I read this letter I was quite sure that my friend had already gone mad. Yet until I knew what was troubling him I would have to do as he asked. I got up at once, sent for a cab, and drove straight to Jekyll's house. The man-servant was waiting for me. He also had had a letter telling him what to do, and he had sent for a carpenter as well as a locksmith. The men came in as Poole and I were speaking, so we all went at once to the old building where Jekyll had his study. The door was very strong, and the lock good. The carpenter said it would take a long time to open and we might even have to break the door down. But the locksmith was a good workman and, although it took him two hours, he was able to open the door. I went in alone. The cupboard with the glass door was unlocked. I took out the drawer, wrapped it in a cloth and brought it to my own house.

I sat down at once to see what was in the drawer. The powders were wrapped up in pieces of paper, and when I opened one of the papers I found a little heap of something like salt. Next I took the bottle from the drawer and found it half-full of a blood-red liquid with a very strong smell. Even though I am a doctor, I could not guess what kind of medicine it was. The notebook had nothing in it except a list of dates. They went back for many years, but I saw that nothing had been written in the book for nearly twelve months.

These things told me nothing, but they made me very puzzled. Here was a bottle with some medicine to drink, a paper or two with some salt-like powder, and an old notebook. How could these things trouble my friend or put his life in danger? Why could his secret messenger not go and get them from his house himself? Why was this man to come to me alone, so late at night?

The more I thought about it, the more sure I was that Henry Jekyll must be mad. I sent my servants off to bed. Then I took out an old gun, loaded it, and put it in my pocket to use if I needed it.

At the very hour of midnight I heard someone knock softly on the door. I went myself to open it and found a small man hiding in the shadows.

"Have you come from Dr Jekyll?" I asked.

"Yes," he said in a whisper. I told him to come in, but first he looked this way and that in the darkness of the street. There was a policeman not far off, and when my visitor saw him he was in a great hurry to come inside.

As I followed him into the light of my room, I kept my hand ready on my gun. Here, at last, I was able to see him clearly. I had never set eyes on him before, I was sure of that. He was small, as I have said. I did not like the look on his face, and his body was twisted in some strange way. There was something wrong with him, something horrible, yet it was hard to tell what it was.

The next thing I noticed was his clothes. They were of good cloth, but far too big for him in every way. The trousers were very wide and the bottoms were rolled up to keep them off the ground. The collar of his coat was far too large and the coat itself too long. It was like a wild animal dressed in the clothes of a man. Who could this be? Where did he come from? What was his life?

All these thoughts passed through my mind in a few moments. My visitor was already jumping about the room like a wild animal.

"Have you got it?" he cried. "Have you got it?"

He was so excited that he even put his hand on my arm and shook me. His touch made my blood run cold.

"Come, sir," said I, "you forget that I do not yet know who you are. Sit down, if you please."

To quieten him I sat down myself in my usual chair and looked at him as if he were a patient.

"I am very sorry, Dr Lanyon," he said. "What you say is quite true, and I have been too quick for you. Yes, I have been sent here by your friend, Dr Henry Jekyll.

It is because . . . I think . . ." He put his hand to his mouth as if he could say no more. He looked like a man about to go mad. "I think . . ." he began again, "there is a drawer . . ."

"There it is, sir," said I, pointing to the drawer where it lay on the floor behind a table. It was still covered with the cloth in which I had wrapped it.

He threw himself at it, and then stopped and put his hand on his heart as if he were about to die there and then. His face was so white that I feared for his life.

"Keep quiet," I said. "There is nothing to fear."

He turned and gave me a horrible look, then pulled away the cloth that covered the drawer. When he saw what was in it he gave a loud cry. Then he asked:

"Have you a drinking-glass?"

I rose from my seat and gave him a glass. He thanked me with a smile, poured out a little of the liquid from the bottle and then put into it one of the white powders. The medicine was red at first, then, as the powder began to break up, it grew lighter and lighter, like a flame of fire. I could hear the noise it made in the drinking-glass as it bubbled in his hand. Then all the bubbling stopped and the liquid changed colour again, growing dark and still. My visitor, who had watched all these changes carefully, smiled again and put the glass down.

"And now," said he, "what are you going to do? Will you listen to me? Will you allow me to take this drinking-glass in my hand and go away from your house without another word? Or are you too interested? Think well before you answer. I shall do as you wish. If you let me go now you shall be left as you were before, and you may go to bed in peace. Or, if you want, you may see the strangest sight in your whole life."

"Sir," I said, trying to keep still, "I do not know what you are talking about, but I have already seen a great deal tonight. I want to see the end of it all."

"That's good," said my visitor. "Lanyon, remember you have given your word. This is a secret between you and me. Now you are about to see a wonder! Watch!"

He put the glass to his lips and drank off the medicine. Then there was a cry, he fell back, caught the table and held on, his eyes wild, his mouth open. As I looked, I saw a change come over him. He seemed to grow bigger, his face grew dark—it was a face I thought I knew!

The next moment I jumped to my feet and fell back against the wall, my arms held out to keep him away.

"O God!" I cried out, "O God!", again and again.

There, before my eyes, shaking all over his body and feeling before him with his hands like a man come back from the dead—there stood Henry Jekyll!

What he told me in the next hour I cannot write down in this letter. It is too horrible. I saw what I saw, I heard what I heard, and it made me afraid. And yet, now that it is all over, I ask myself if I really believe that it happened, and I cannot answer. My life is nearly gone, I cannot sleep, I am afraid by day and by night. I am sure the end is near and that I am going to die. I will say but one thing more, Utterson. The visitor who came into my house that night was, as Jekyll told me, the man known by the name of Hyde. He was the man everyone is looking for—the murderer of Carew.

HASTIE LANYON.

That was the end of the letter.

10

Henry Jekyll's Own Story

Mr Utterson then opened the envelope with the papers from Dr Jekyll. This is what he read:

I was born in the year 18— into a good home with plenty of money and every chance to grow up to a life of useful work. I must say that when I was a boy I was as happy as anyone could be. I liked to work hard and I wanted to please my fellow-men. But it was not long before I felt that there were two people inside me. One of them wished to be quiet and good in the company of older people and to be well thought of by them. The other liked to be noisy, naughty, and often very wicked. So I learned very early that a man is not one person, but two. In other words, he may have one face and voice for the people he meets day by day. But he may have very different thoughts and words when he is alone.

I used to dream about it. If only, I told myself, I could cut myself in two! Then the bad man in me could go his own way and do what he liked without making any trouble for the good and kind part of me. The good side of me, on the other hand, could go about doing good things and be happy without bothering about his twin who was such a rascal. At times all of us must have felt like that. Many a day the bad and the good have fought one another inside us. If only they could be cut into two different people and go their own way!

I thought about it many a time as I grew up and went to my medical classes at the hospital. When I became a doctor I spent a lot of time trying to find a drug or medicine which would set free the two men inside my one body. At last I thought I had it.

I waited a long time before I tried it out. I knew that what I was about to drink might kill me, for any drug so strong that it could change my whole body and mind must be very dangerous. Why, it might not only change me—it might put an end to me at once! But I could not leave it alone. I wanted to do it. I must do it. Long before this I had bought part of the medicine I needed, a large amount of a drug which looked like salt. Then, late one night, I mixed this drug and liquid together and watched them boiling and bubbling in the glass. When the whole thing had stopped bubbling I took up the glass and drank the medicine.

The next thing I knew was terrible pain which spread all over my body. Every part of me, from head to foot, burned and shook with fever. I was very sick and felt as if I were about to die. Then everything about me seemed to grow dark, and I came to myself as if I were waking up from a deep sleep. It was a strange feeling. I felt younger, lighter, happier in moving my arms and legs and whole body. My mind was free to think about anything in the world. At the same time I knew that I was wicked through and through, and I was glad at the thought! I waved my hands above my head, happy as a boy at play. As I did so, I knew all at once that I was much smaller from head to foot.

There was no mirror in my room at that time. The one which stands there now was brought there much later on so that I might see what was happening every time I took the medicine. That first night, however, my one thought was to see what I looked like. I left my study, hurried across the courtyard and went up to my bedroom in the house. In the mirror there I saw for the first time the shape of Edward Hyde.

This was the evil side of my nature, not so strong at that time as the good part. I think that is why it came about that Edward Hyde was so much smaller, thinner and younger than Henry Jekyll. Yet when I looked at that ugly, twisted thing in the mirror I was not afraid or sorry. This person was part of me, and I was glad. He looked real and alive and much better in my eyes than the double person I seemed to be day by day. I have often noticed that when I went about as Edward Hyde, no one wanted to come near me or touch me. It was as if they were afraid. I think this is because all people, as we see them, are a mixture of good and bad. Edward Hyde alone was all evil, and everyone could feel it.

I did not stand long before the mirror that night. I had still to find out if I could change back into my other shape, the good Henry Jekyll. If not, then I would have to run away before morning from the house that was no longer mine. I hurried back to my study, mixed the drug again and quickly drank it off. Once again I felt great pain in every part of my body. When I came to myself, there was the nature, the shape, and the face of Henry Jekyll once more.

That night I knew that I had come to the cross-roads of my life. In that evil time all I had wanted to do was to set free the shape of Edward Hyde. Now I knew that I had two natures as well as two different bodies. One was all evil, in the shape of Hyde. The other was still the old Henry Jekyll, that man who was a mixture of good and bad like all other people in the world.

Even at that time I did not want to spend all my evenings in my study reading books. What a dull life that would be! I wanted to enjoy myself, to play like a boy. Yet, how could I do that when everyone knew me as Henry Jekyll, a busy doctor in the town of London, and far too old for such silly play? It was in this way that the new drug took hold of me. I had only to drink the glass of medicine, put off at once the body of the well-known doctor, and put on, like a coat, the body of

Edward Hyde. I smiled to think of it, it was so easy. Then I made my plans with great care.

I bought that house in Soho where the police hunted for Hyde. I furnished it well so that I could live there any time I wanted. I was able to find a servant to look after it for me, a woman, you remember, who was as strange and as evil as Hyde himself. Here, in my own home, I told all my servants that a Mr Hyde was to come and go as he liked and to make himself at home at any time. I told them what he looked like, and, to be quite sure that all was well, I went to my own house one day in the shape of Hyde. I found that the servants did as I had told them. Then I wrote out that will which you did not like, so that if anything should happen to Dr Jekyll I would get the money and the house and everything in the name of Edward Hyde. So, with all my plans made, I began to enjoy my strange double life.

Many a time men have paid other men to do wrong for them, to kill and to steal while they themselves were safe. But I am the first man ever to do these things as if they were a game to be played. I was the first who could go about every day as the doctor who was well known and liked by everyone, and, in an instant, like a school-boy, change my clothes and become another man. I was quite safe in my new shape. Think of it—there was no such person as Edward Hyde! Once I was safe in my study, give me only a second or two to mix and drink the drug I had always standing ready—then, whatever evil he had done, Edward Hyde would go from sight like a breath on a mirror. There, in his place, quietly at home among his books, was Dr Henry Jekyll. No one could ever speak ill of *him*!

At first I did things that were as silly as the games of a young boy. But in the shape of Edward Hyde it was not long before I turned to real evil. When I came back from these terrible evenings I used to wonder at what I had done. This man Hyde whom I set free to do as he liked had no bit of good in him at all. He could do only wrong. Every thought and act was for himself. He loved to bring trouble to others. Henry Jekyll stood afraid before the horrible acts of Edward Hyde. On the other hand, why should he blame himself? It was Hyde, and Hyde alone, who was in the wrong. Jekyll did not get any worse. When he came to himself he seemed quite unchanged. He even tried, when he could, to undo the evil done by Hyde. So the two different men went their own way, the one good, the other bad.

One evil, however, leads to another. I put myself in danger one night, my dear Utterson, when I was seen by a friend of yours. A horrible thing I did to a child made an angry passer-by run after me—it was your young friend and cousin, Mr Enfield. The doctor and the child's family joined him, and they were so angry that I was afraid for my life. At last, in order to keep them quiet Edward Hyde had to bring them to the door in the side street and pay them by a cheque signed by Henry Jekyll. Yes, that was a great danger, since it brought our names together. In case it should happen again I put some money in another bank in the name of Edward Hyde himself. I held the pen in a different way so that the writing did not look like Jekyll's. This would be Hyde's way of writing in time to come. Surely now I was safe, and Dr Jekyll and Mr Hyde were both free to do what they liked!

11

The End of Henry Jekyll

Mr Utterson sat on in his office still reading Henry Jekyll's long letter. His story went on :

About two months before the murder of Sir Danvers Carew I had been out one night on one of my adventures in the shape of Edward Hyde. I came home late, drank off the drug, and woke up the next day in bed feeling very strange. What was wrong ? I looked about me. The bedroom and furniture were the same as they always had been. The bed was mine, and the bed-clothes, and the curtains on the window which I saw every morning when I woke. Yet all the time I felt sure that there was something wrong. Surely I had not wakened where I seemed to be, but in the little room in Soho where I sometimes slept in the body of Edward Hyde ? I smiled to myself, knowing that the thought was silly. There was no doubt that I was in my own house. My eyes told me that.

All at once I caught sight of my hand. Now you will remember, my dear Utterson, that the hand of Henry Jekyll was large, white, and well-shaped—the hand of a doctor, without a doubt. But the hand which I now saw clearly enough in the morning light was thin, bony, dark yellow in colour and with thick black hair on the back. It was the hand of Edward Hyde.

I must have looked at it for nearly half a minute, wondering what on earth had happened. Then I was wide-awake in a moment. Fear took hold of me and, jumping from my bed, I rushed to the mirror. At the sight that met my eyes my blood ran thin and cold as ice. Yes, I had gone to bed Henry Jekyll, but I had woken up Edward Hyde.

How had this happened, and what was to be done? All my drugs were in the study, a long way off—downstairs from my bedroom, through the hall, across the open courtyard, and upstairs to my room in the other building. I could cover my face so that no one would know me. But what use was that? I could not hide the change in my height and shape.

Suddenly I remembered that the servants were already used to the coming and going of my second self. It would be all right. I dressed as well as I could in the clothes that were too big for me and set out for my study. Ten minutes later Dr Jekyll had come back to his own shape and was sitting down to breakfast in his own home, as if nothing had happened.

I was no longer hungry. I could not understand what had gone wrong, no matter how much I tried to think it out. Then I began to wonder about the days to come. Would I be able to go on living as two different men, changing easily from one to the other? It seemed to me that the body of Edward Hyde had grown a little, as though he were trying to become bigger and stronger than Henry Jekyll. Was it possible that soon I might not be able to change back to my usual body? Perhaps the day was near when I should always be Hyde and never again Jekyll.

I could not always trust the drug. Once, many months before, it had not worked at all. More than once I had had to mix twice the usual amount of the drug, and once, at the risk of death, to take the stuff three times. Now I thought again of what had happened that morning. It looked as if the drug were becoming too weak to let me come back to my usual shape. I was losing my better self. The evil part of me was not willing to let go.

I knew that I had to choose between the two men. It was now or never. But how hard it was to make up my mind! The part of me that was Jekyll knew all about Hyde and wanted him to go on having his adventures, evil though they were. Hyde, on the other hand, cared nothing at all about Jekyll and never wanted to go back to the doctor's shape. If I chose to be Jekyll alone from this time onwards, I could no longer enjoy any secret adventures night after night. If, on the other hand, I chose to be Hyde, then I would be a man for ever without friends, lonely and hated. Which part of me was I to be —the good or the bad?

I made up my mind. Yes, I would be the kindly old doctor with his pleasant home, his daily work, and his good friends. I would say goodbye for ever to the younger man with his quick step and all the excitement of his life.

For two months I kept my word to myself. Then, all of a sudden, I felt like a thirsty man crying out for something to drink. Inside me Hyde was fighting to be free. At last, in a weak moment, I made up the medicine again and drank the liquid in the glass.

I don't think I knew even then the danger I was in. Edward Hyde came out like an animal that had been kept too long in a cage. He—no, it was I—was wild with evil.

3

That was the night I met Sir Danvers Carew. Only for a moment or two did I listen to the words of that kind old man when he stopped to speak to me in the lane. Then I knocked him down like a child breaking a toy.

It was only when I grew tired hitting his body with my stick that I knew what I had done. Fear swept through me. I saw that my life was in danger, and I turned and ran from the horrible place. I ran to the house in Soho and, to make quite sure, burned every paper I could find that had the name of Edward Hyde on it. Then I set out through the lamplit streets, half of my mind filled with joy at my crime, the other half afraid that someone would find me out. Hyde had a song on his lips as he drank the drug that night. The next moment Henry Jekyll was there on his knees, sorry for what he had done and crying out for God's help. I looked back on my whole life. I remembered the time when I was a little child and held my father's hand, then the days when I was a student learning to be a doctor. What had I come to? Again and again the horrible thought of the past night filled my mind. My crime stared me in the face.

One thing was plain now. I must never be Hyde again. How happy I was to think that! I locked the door into the side street by which I had so often gone in and out as Edward Hyde. I threw the key to the ground and broke it. Never again would I need to use it!

Next day came the news that a servant girl had seen the murder and that everyone knew it was Hyde who had done it. In a way I was glad to hear the news. Now I must be Jekyll for ever. If Hyde showed his face even for a moment, all hands would be ready to take him and put him to death.

So the days and weeks went by. You know yourself, my dear Utterson, how hard I worked for others in the last months of last year. The days passed quietly, almost happily for me, busy as I was in my medical work among the sick and suffering. But even in those happy days I was still two people, and the more Hyde was shut up the more he cried out to be set free.

There comes an end to all things. It was a fine, clear January day. The streets were wet after the rain, but the sky was shining overhead. Regent's Park in the middle of London was full of birds singing their sweet songs, and the flowers were opening with the coming of spring. I sat there in the sun and thought about the past. After all, I thought to myself, perhaps I was no worse than other people. I had done a great deal of good in my busy life as a doctor. Why should I not enjoy my evil thoughts now and again if I wanted to?

At that very moment I felt as sick as death, and my body shook all over. I looked down. My clothes hung loosely on my thin legs and arms and the hand that lay on my knee was bony and hairy. I was once more Edward Hyde. A moment before I had been safe—loved and liked by everyone. Now I was a hunted man without a home, a murderer who ought to be put to death.

Hyde's mind was always quick and sharp. I was not caught yet. My drugs were in one of the cupboards in my study. How was I to get at them? I sat there and tried to think of a plan. I had shut the side door and locked it, and the key was broken. There was no hope that way. If I tried to go in by the front door of the house my own servants would lay hands on me at once. They all knew about Hyde and his crimes now. I saw that I must use someone else, and thought of Lanyon. How could I reach him? Even if I were not caught in the streets, how could I ever get into his house? And how could I, Edward Hyde, beg the good doctor to break into the study of his friend Henry Jekyll?

Then I remembered there was one thing I could still do in the part of Dr Jekyll. I could still write a letter as the doctor used to do. I saw what I must try. I got up, pulled my clothes round me as best I could, called a passing cab, and drove to a hotel not far away. The driver of the cab laughed at the first sight of me, but he shook with terror when he saw my face and did what he was told. At the hotel as I went in I looked so wild that the servants were quick to do what they were told at once and get out of my way. They took me to a room where I could be alone and brought me paper, pen, and ink. Hyde in danger of his life was a new person, even to me. He shook with anger and wanted to knock down everyone he saw, but he forced himself to be quiet and wrote his two letters. One, as you know, was to Lanyon, and the other to Poole. Then he called a servant and sent them out to be posted.

After that Edward Hyde sat all day beside the fire in that lonely room. He dined there, alone with his fears. Then, when the night was quite dark, he set out in a cab and told the driver to take him to and fro about the streets of the city.

He, I say—I cannot say I. He was no longer like a man. Nothing lived in him now but fear and hate. At last he left the cab and went on foot in his strange clothes, like a wild animal of the night. He walked fast, talking to himself, counting the minutes that he had to wait until midnight.

When at last I drank the drug and came to myself in Lanyon's house I could see the horror in the face of my old friend. A change had come over me. I was no longer afraid of being caught by the police and put to death as a murderer. It was the thought of being Hyde that filled me with fear. Almost in a dream I listened to what Lanyon had to say. Partly in a dream I came home to my own house and got into bed. I fell into a deep sleep at once and when I woke in the morning all was well. I still hated and feared the animal that was in me, and I had not forgotten the dangers of the day before. But I was at home again, and near my drugs. Surely I was safe?

I was walking across the courtyard after breakfast that morning, enjoying the fresh air, when all of a sudden my body began to shake with the change that was about to happen. I had time only to run to my study and shut the door before I was again in the evil shape of Hyde. This time it took a double dose of the drug to bring me back to Henry Jekyll. Alas, six hours later, as I sat sadly by the fire, the same thing happened again, and I had to take more of the drug. Indeed, from that day on I had to take more and more of the stuff and fight with all my mind to keep the shape of Henry Jekyll. At all hours of the day and night it would happen. Above all, if I went to sleep it was always as Hyde that I woke up.

I tried to keep myself from sleep altogether, but that could not be. I became sick and weak in body and mind, with only one thought: the horror of my other self. When I did sleep for a little, or when the drug wore off, I changed in a moment into the twisted body and evil mind of Hyde. He was as strong now as Jekyll was weak. They came to hate one another. Jekyll thought of Hyde as something horrible and cruel that he had made with the drug. It was like a deadly sickness lying inside his body, eating away his life. Hyde, too, hated Jekyll. In his own shape he would rush about the room tearing my books to bits, burning my letters, breaking the picture of my father that hung on the wall. He is afraid of only one thing. He fears that I will kill myself and so kill him.

I have little more to tell you, Utterson. This might have gone on for years, but the drug which I needed came to an end. I sent Poole for some more, and mixed the drink again. I drank it, but this time it did not do its work. You will hear from Poole how he searched all over London for the right stuff. It was useless.

About a week has passed, and I am now finishing this letter in the shape of Henry Jekyll for the last time. My drugs are all finished. This is the last time that Henry Jekyll can think his own thoughts for a moment or two and see his own sad face in the mirror. If I begin to change my shape as I go on writing, Hyde will tear this letter in pieces. But how can I know what will happen before you read this—if ever you do?

The end of Edward Hyde, too, is near. Half an hour or so from now, when I shall again and for ever become Hyde, I shall wait for the sound of the police. Will Hyde die as a murderer, paying for his crimes? Or will he be brave enough to kill himself before this room is broken into? God knows. This is the moment when Henry Jekyll dies and Hyde takes his place. Here, then, as I lay down the pen and close this letter, I bring the story of that unhappy Henry Jekyll to an end.

THE SUICIDE CLUB

"New Arabian Nights", the series of stories that includes *The Suicide Club*, was first published in 1878 in the short-lived weekly journal *London*. This was one of Robert Louis Stevenson's first attempts at a story set in his own time. Before that he had only written essays or historical studies, and books of travel.

Even so, the "New Arabian Nights" themselves contained more of fantasy than of real life. It seems that Robert Louis's cousin, Robert Alan Stevenson, suggested the idea of the story of *The Suicide Club* to him, and the Young Man with the Cream Tarts is supposed to represent Robert Alan himself.

It is clear that the cousins did not mean the story to be taken too seriously, but it certainly does expose the evils of gambling, about which Robert Louis felt strongly, as well as the moral danger of having too much money to spend and too little work to do. And Robert Louis Stevenson shows himself to be already a first-class writer of suspense stories, especially in the scene where the fatal cards are being dealt.

EXERCISES

1. Can you guess why Robert Louis Stevenson called this series of stories "New Arabian Nights"?

2. Do you think the author agreed with his cousin's light-hearted argument that people should commit suicide in order to reach paradise more quickly? What are the reasons for your answer?

3. What parts of the story do you consider most "fantastic", and why?

1

The Young Man with the Cream Tarts

Prince Florizel of Bohemia was a man who loved adventure, wherever he might find it. One evening in the month of March he and his friend Colonel Geraldine were sitting in a bar in the heart of London, listening to the talk and watching all that went on. Both men were dressed in old clothes which made them look poor and plain. The Prince had even added false whiskers and eyebrows to his face so that no one would know him.

The bar was full of men and women eating and drinking. All at once the door swung open and a young man followed by two servants pushed his way through the crowd. Each of the servants carried a large dish of cream tarts which the young man tried to give away one by one to anyone who would take them. Some people laughed and took a tart. Perhaps they thought he was a little mad. Others said no, and told him to go away. When that happened he ate the tart himself.

At last he came to Prince Florizel.

"Sir," said he with a low bow, "will you take this from a stranger?" He held out a tart. "I can tell you that it is good, for I have eaten twenty-seven of them since five o'clock."

The Prince held out his hand. "If my friend and I eat your tarts," he said, "you must sit down and tell us why you are doing this."

The young man thought for a moment. "Very well," he said. "But first you must follow me to other bars until I have given away every tart. Then I shall tell you all about it."

The Prince and Colonel Geraldine each ate a tart and rose to their feet. Arm in arm they followed the young man and his servants. At last, after they had visited two more bars, their leader counted his tarts. There were nine left, three in one dish and six in the other.

"Gentlemen," he said, "I must not keep you waiting any longer." With these words he took the nine tarts and put them in his mouth, one after the other. Then he emptied his purse into the hands of the two servants and sent them away.

"Follow me if you will," he said to the Prince and Colonel Geraldine. "I have spent every penny giving away these tarts. This is perhaps my last night alive. I am on my way to the Suicide Club!"

"The Suicide Club?" said the Prince. "Why, what the devil is that?"

"It is a door to death," answered the young man. "If, like me, you are tired of life, I will take you to a meeting where men are sure to find death. What do you say?"

The two men looked at one another. Then the Prince whispered to his friend.

"We must go with him," he said, "and save him. But remember, no one is to know who I really am. We must use different names—I shall call myself Mr Godall, and you will be Major Alfred Hammersmith."

He turned to the young man. "Lead on, sir!" he cried. "I am not the man to turn back from an adventure."

A few minutes later a cab took them to a dark house in a quiet street. After Colonel Geraldine had paid the fare, the young man turned and spoke to Prince Florizel.

"There is still time to run away, Mr Godall. And you, too, Major Hammersmith. As for me, I have said goodbye to life. But think well before you take another step. Death lies before you!"

The Prince waved him on. "I am not afraid," he said.

"Follow me, then," was the answer. "The President will see you in his room. You must be straight and truthful or he will not let you join the club."

No one stopped them as they went in. The outer door was wide open. The young man led them to a small room and left them there. From next door the two men could hear the sound of talk and laughter where, no doubt, the club was meeting. The room they were in had very little furniture, but the hats and coats that hung on pegs all round the walls showed that there must be many people in the house.

"What sort of a place is this?" said Geraldine.

"That is what I have come to see," answered Prince Florizel. "It sounds like a house for devils."

A door opened quietly and the President of the Suicide Club came in. He was a man of fifty or so, large and slow-moving, with side-whiskers, a bald head, and grey eyes. He looked coldly at the strangers.

"Good evening," said he, after he had closed the door behind him. "I am told that you wish to speak with me."

"We want to join the Suicide Club, sir," replied the Colonel.

"Sir," said the President, "you have made a mistake. This is my own house, and you must leave it at once."

The Prince sat quietly in his seat. "I have come here," said he, "with a friend of yours who told me I could join your club. I am a very peaceful man usually, but, my dear sir, you must let me stay, or I will make trouble."

The President laughed loudly.

"That is the way to speak," said he. "I see you are a man who is a man. I believe in you."

The Prince and the Colonel had to answer many questions about themselves; this they did as if they were in fact Mr Godall and Major Hammersmith. Then the President made them promise to keep the rules of the club, and Florizel and Geraldine both signed a paper. They paid the President a sum of money and at last he led the way from the room into the meeting of the Suicide Club.

The room which they came into was large and well lit. There were eighteen people there, most of them smoking and drinking. They were all men, and they seemed very excited and laughed a lot.

Prince Florizel at once began to go here and there about the room, talking to the members of the club in the easy, happy way which was his nature. As he went from one to another he kept his eyes and ears open. Most of the men were young, but none of them looked either strong or wise. Indeed, it seemed a half-mad company. They stood leaning on tables and moving their feet, unable to be still for a moment. They talked a great deal, but without much sense. Some of them had a great deal to say about terrible things they had done and why they wanted to die soon. They spoke easily about death, as if it were nothing, and yet many of them were white-faced and afraid. Prince Florizel did not think much of any of them.

"If a man has made up his mind to kill himself," he thought, "let him do it without all this noise and talk."

Meanwhile Geraldine had met an older man who sat quietly in a corner by himself. He was as thin as skin and bone could be, and looked as if he had been ill for many years. His name, the President told the Colonel, was Mr Malthus. When the Colonel spoke to him, Mr Malthus told him to sit down beside him.

"You are a new-comer?" he said. "You want to hear about the club? Well, I can tell you, for I have been a member for two years."

The Colonel was surprised. If Mr Malthus had come

to this place for two years there could be little danger for the Prince in one evening.

"What!" he cried. "Is it all a joke? Two years! How does that come about?"

"I do not come every evening," answered Mr Malthus, "only about once a month. I have been ill quite often, and that has kept me away. But I have also been very lucky. I cannot stay away, yet I am afraid to come here. You see, I am a coward, and I play with fear."

"You will have to tell me what happens in the club," said the Colonel. "You must remember that I have just come."

"An ordinary member who comes here looking for death," said Mr Malthus, "must come back every evening until he finds what he wants. The President is always here. The others must go when their turn comes to die. It is the President who deals the cards."

"Deals the cards?" said the Colonel. "What do you mean?"

"Every evening a victim is chosen," answered Mr Malthus, "and not only a victim, but also another member who must put him to death. It is all very interesting."

"Good God!" said the Colonel, "do they kill each other?"

"It is much easier than suicide," said Mr Malthus with a smile.

"And may you—may I—may my friend—may any one of us be chosen this evening to kill another man? Is that what you mean?" The Colonel was filled with horror. He got to his feet as if he wished to run away as fast as he could.

At that moment he caught sight of Prince Florizel looking across the room at him. The Colonel remembered why they had come.

"After all," he said lightly, "why not? Since you say the game is interesting, I look forward to seeing it!"

"Give me your arm and help me to the table," said Mr Malthus. "I see that the game is about to begin."

Another door was opened at that moment and all the members of the club went through into the next room. In the middle was a long green table at which the President sat with a pack of cards in his hands.

Mr Malthus could move so slowly that everyone was seated before he and the Colonel and the Prince sat down side by side.

"It is a pack of fifty-two cards," whispered Mr Malthus. "Watch for the ace of spades. That is the sign of death. And then look for the ace of clubs. The man who gets that must do the crime. Happy, happy young men," he added. One of them must die tonight!"

The Colonel told the Prince in a whisper all he had heard from Mr Malthus. They both felt their blood run cold at what was about to happen. But they could not escape now.

"We must play the game to the end," said the Prince. He looked about him at the others. The members of the club were all very quiet. Everyone was frightened, but none so frightened as Mr Malthus, in spite of his words. His hand was at his mouth, his head shook, and his lips were white.

"Now, gentlemen," said the President. He began slowly to give out the cards one by one round the table, waiting until each man had turned over his card to see what it was. Nearly everyone was slow. Some of them seemed afraid to touch the card at all. When the Prince's turn came he could feel his heart beating fast within him. The card he got was the nine of clubs. Colonel Geraldine had the three of spades. Mr Malthus turned over the queen of hearts, and cried out with joy that he was safe. The young man of the cream tarts came next. He turned over the ace of clubs, and his face was full of horror. He had not come there to kill, but to be killed. This was a terrible thing he had to do!

Once again the cards came round, and still the card of death had not come out. The players held their breath. Which of them was to die that very night? The Prince had another club, and Geraldine had a diamond. Both were safe, for the moment. Then there was a sudden noise beside them, a cry from Mr Malthus as he turned up his card. It was the ace of spades! His luck, as he called it, had changed at last. He was to die!

At once everyone began to talk again. The players got up from the table and walked in twos and threes into the other room to smoke and have another drink. The President stood up and yawned loudly, like a man who had done a good day's work. But Mr Malthus sat in his place with his head in his hands, as still as if he were already dead.

Prince Florizel and Colonel Geraldine went from the room at once.

"Call a cab," said the Prince. "Let us get away and try to forget this horrible night."

The next morning, as soon as the Prince was awake, Colonel Geraldine brought him a newspaper. This is what he read:

"SAD ACCIDENT

This morning, about two o'clock, Mr Bartholomew Malthus, of 16 Chepstow Place, Westbourne Grove, on his way home from a party at a friend's house, fell over the wall in Trafalgar Square and broke his skull as well as a leg and an arm. He died at once. Mr Malthus had been ill for a long time and was able to walk only very slowly. It is thought that he must have fallen before anyone could save him. Everyone who knew him will be sorry to hear of his death."

The Prince was silent, his head in his hands.

"I cannot feel sorry for Malthus," said the Colonel. "He played a game with fear and loved to see others go to their death. But I am very sorry for our young man of the cream tarts."

"Geraldine," said the Prince, raising his head, "that unhappy young man did this terrible thing. But the man to blame for it all is the President. When I think of him my heart grows sick within me. Some day I shall punish that man. I swear it!"

"You mean to go back to the club?" cried the Colonel. "Think of the danger! I beg you not to go!"

"I have thought about it," said Prince Florizel. "But you must remember why we went to the club in the first place—to help that unhappy young man we met last night. Now he needs our help more than ever. Can I leave the President to go on his evil way? No, Geraldine. Tonight, once more, we take our places at the table of the Suicide Club. Do what you like today, but be here before eleven o'clock this evening in the same clothes."

The club, on this second evening, was not so busy as the night before. When Geraldine and the Prince came in there were only six or seven people in the room. Prince Florizel spoke to the President about the death early that morning.

The President smiled. "Poor Malthus," he said. "The club will not be the same without him. Most of the others are little more than boys, sir. They are poor company for me, and they go very soon. Mr Malthus was an old friend."

The young man of the cream tarts sat in a corner of the room, looking very sad. The Prince and the Colonel tried to speak to him.

"How I wish I had never brought you here!" he cried. "It is a horrible place. Go away, I beg you, before you have to kill. Oh, if you could have heard the old man scream as he fell, and the noise of his bones breaking! I shall never forget it. There is only one thing I wish— the ace of spades tonight!"

A few more members came in as the evening went on, but there were not more than thirteen altogether when they took their places at the table. The Prince once again felt very much afraid as he sat down. He saw, however, that his friend Geraldine seemed to be quite happy.

"Strange," he thought. "It was he who begged me not to come."

"Now, gentlemen," said the President, and he began to give out the cards.

Three times the cards went all round the table and yet neither of the cards of death had come out. As the President began to go round the table for the fourth time, everyone was waiting and watching. They must

come out, this time. The Prince was sitting where he would get the second last card. The third player turned up a black ace—it was the ace of clubs. The next had a diamond, the next a heart, and so on, but there was no sign yet of the ace of spades. At last Geraldine, who sat beside the Prince, turned over his card. It was an ace, but the ace of hearts.

When Prince Florizel looked at the table in front of him his heart stood still. He was a brave man, but now the sweat ran down his face. There were only two cards left. One of them must be the card of death. He turned over the card before him. It was the ace of spades!

The Prince heard the player at his side burst into a loud laugh. He saw the other members of the club rise from their seats and walk away, but he sat still, thinking of other things. He saw how silly he had been, playing this deadly game for the sake of an hour's adventure.

"God," he cried, "God help me!"

When he stood up he found to his surprise that Geraldine was not in the room. The man who was to kill him was there, talking to the President, learning what he was to do. The young man of the cream tarts came up to the Prince and whispered in his ear.

"I would give a million pounds, if I had it, for your luck," he told him.

The other two had stopped talking. The man who held the ace of clubs left the room as if he were ready for anything. The President came over to the Prince and shook his hand.

"I am glad to have met you, sir," said he, "and to be able to help you in this way. At least you cannot say that you have had long to wait. On the second evening— what a lucky man you are!"

The Prince tried to say something, but his mouth was dry, and he could not speak a word.

"You feel a little sick?" asked the President. "Most gentlemen do. Will you take a little brandy?"

The Prince nodded his head, and the other at once poured some brandy into a glass.

"Poor old Malthus!" said the President as the Prince drank it. "He took nearly a bottle of brandy last night, but it did not seem to do him much good!"

"I feel better now," said the Prince. "Tell me at once what I am to do."

"You are to walk along the Strand towards the City," said the President, "and on the left-hand side of the road. After a little while you will meet the gentleman who has just left the room—the one who holds the ace of clubs. He will tell you what you are to do next, and you will listen to him in every way. And now," added the President, "I wish you a pleasant walk."

Florizel bowed and left the room without another word. He went through the room where most of the players were still smoking and drinking, but he did not look to right or to left. He put on his hat and coat and laughed at the thought that it was for the last time.

"Come, come, I must be a man," he thought. "I shall go on my way and meet my death as bravely as I can." He went out through the open door into the dark street.

At the corner of the road, only a few steps from the house, three men jumped out of the darkness and caught Prince Florizel. They held his arms so that he could not fight, then pushed him inside a carriage which came along at that instant. It drove away at a great speed. When Florizel sat up he found there was already someone in the carriage.

"Will your Highness pardon me?" said a well-known voice.

The Prince laughed and threw his arms round Colonel Geraldine.

"How can I ever thank you?" he cried. "How did you do it?"

"You can thank me by keeping away from such danger," said the Colonel. "As for your other question —I ordered your own servants to watch that house from the time we came there this evening. This is one of your own carriages which has been waiting for you."

"And the unhappy man who was to kill me—what of him?" asked the Prince.

"He was caught as he left the club," answered the Colonel, "and now waits for you at the Palace. Soon the other members of the Suicide Club will be brought there also. I have given orders that that is to be done."

An hour later Prince Florizel of Bohemia, dressed in his finest clothes, met the members of the Suicide Club in a room in his Palace.

"You wicked men," he said to them, "some of you have joined this club because you were poor and had no work to do. My officers will find work for you, so that you may live and earn your living. I am sorry for all of you. Tomorrow you shall tell me your stories and I shall try to help you, each one.

"As for you," he added, turning to the President, "I shall not try to help you. Here"—the Prince laid his hand on the shoulder of Colonel Geraldine's young brother—"is an officer of mine who is about to go a short journey on the Continent. You are to go with him."

The Prince looked hard at the President and when he spoke again it was in a low voice.

"Do you shoot well with a pistol?" he asked. "You will have to do that if you go with this officer of mine. And let me tell you that if anything happens to young Mr Geraldine, I shall always have another officer to send after you. Remember, my arm is long!"

That was the last the members of the Suicide Club saw of one another. The Prince found work for them as he had said, and the President went on his way with Mr Geraldine and two of the Prince's servants. Mr Geraldine was known to be a very good shot. No one expected ever to see the President of the Suicide Club again.

2

Duel to the Death

Lieutenant Brackenbury Rich was a soldier who had fought bravely in the Indian Wars. It was many years since he had been in London, and as he went for a walk one evening he felt that he was a stranger in a great town of four million people. The evening was already dark and soon the rain began to fall. By good luck, however, a cab stopped beside him and the driver opened the door. Brackenbury got in and sat down.

"Where to, sir?" asked the driver.

"Where you please," said Brackenbury.

At once the cab went off at a good speed. They went through street after street until Brackenbury felt quite lost. At last the cab stopped in front of a large house with lights in every window. There seemed to be other people arriving and many servants about the place.

"Here we are, sir," said the driver.

"Here!" answered Brackenbury. "Where?"

"You told me to take you where I pleased, sir," said the man with a laugh, "and here we are. My orders were to bring here any gentleman who would come, especially officers of the army, as I guess you are. All you have to do is to go to the door and say that Mr Morris asked you to come."

"Are you Mr Morris?" asked the Lieutenant.

"Oh, no," said the cabman. "Mr Morris is the man who owns that house."

"A strange way to meet someone I have never even heard of," said Brackenbury. "If I say I won't go in, what then?"

"My orders are to drive you back where I took you from," said the man, "and to go and look for others. Those who do not like adventure, Mr Morris said, are not the men for him."

At that the Lieutenant made up his mind.

"I will go and see what he wants," he said. "I am ready for any adventure."

The front door was wide open and a servant met Brackenbury at once and took his coat and hat. Then he led him upstairs where another servant asked his name and showed him into a room full of people.

"Lieutenant Brackenbury Rich!" he called out, and a young man came up to him at once. It was Mr Morris himself.

"I have heard a great deal about you, Lieutenant Rich," he said with a smile. "The newspapers have been full of the brave things you have done. You must pardon the strange way you have been brought to my house. Come and have something to eat and enjoy yourself, I beg you."

The Lieutenant ate a good meal and drank some good wine. But all the time he was thinking: "Who is this Mr Morris? Why does he bring strangers from the streets to his house?" It was plain that the other people in the room had come there in the same way. In fact, the cabs were still coming and going at the front door.

As the evening went on the place grew quieter. At

last a servant took Brackenbury to a smaller room where there were only four other people. Mr Morris welcomed him with a smile and asked him to sit down.

"It is now time, gentlemen, to tell you why you have been asked to come here. I need your help in a most dangerous adventure. I know, of course, that we have not met before, and I must beg you to keep this evening a secret. If any of you wish to go home, now is the time to do it."

A very tall dark man got to his feet.

"Thank you, sir," he said. "I want nothing more to do with you or your house, though you have been kind enough this evening. I am going home to bed."

"You are quite right," said Mr Morris. "I spoke of danger, and if you have no taste for it, then go, by all means."

Another man got up when he heard this, and the two went out together. The only people who sat still were Brackenbury and a red-nosed army Major. They showed no sign of fear, but waited to hear what was to happen next.

"I have chosen my men like Joshua in the Bible," said Mr Morris, "and now I believe I have the best in London. I have been watching you all evening, and I see that a call to danger does not frighten you away."

"Those other two ran away quickly enough," said the Major, "but we will stand by you, whatever it is you want us to do. Lieutenant Rich," he went on, holding out his hand, "I have heard much about you. My name is Major O'Rooke. Now I must ask Mr Morris one thing —is it a duel?"

"A duel to the death," was the reply. "Now you must

call me Morris no longer. Call me Hammersmith, if you please. It is not my real name. I am an officer like your-selves, and I serve a nobleman who is in great danger. Three days ago he went away in a hurry from his home and until this morning I did not know where he had gone. One thing I do know—he is hunting for a wicked man who was President of a club of unhappy and silly men. Already two of our friends, one of them my own dear brother, have been killed by this evil man. Now it is my master or this man—one of them will die. But my noble master still lives. Read this letter which came from him only this morning."

(As the reader knows, the speaker was Colonel Geraldine, and he was talking about Prince Florizel and the President of the Suicide Club.)

The letter said :

"MAJOR HAMMERSMITH,

On Wednesday, at three o'clock in the morning, you will go to the small door that leads into the gardens of Rochester House, Regent's Park. Be there in time. Bring my box of swords, and, if you can find them, one or two gentlemen who are brave and who are sure to help you. Choose men who do not know me, and do not tell them who I really am.

T. GODALL."

"You two gentlemen are the bravest I can find in London," said Colonel Geraldine. "I know you will help me. Will you come ?"

"During a long life," answered Major O'Rooke, "I never took back my hand from anything. Let us go!"

Brackenbury said the same. The Colonel gave each of them a loaded pistol and the three men got into a cab and drove off through the night.

Rochester House was an old building on the banks of the canal with a large garden all round it. There was no sign of a light anywhere, and the whole place looked as if it had been empty for many a year.

The cab was sent away, and the three men soon found the small door in the wall round the garden. There they were to wait. It was nearly three o'clock, very dark, and the rain was falling heavily. They spoke in whispers to one another, wondering what was to happen. All at once Geraldine raised his hand and signed to the others to be quiet. Through the noise of the rain they heard the steps and voices of two men from the other side of the high wall.

"Is the grave dug?" asked one.

"It is," said the other, "behind these bushes here. When the job is done we can cover it up."

The first speaker laughed. "In an hour from now," he said. Then, by the sound of the steps, the listeners knew that they had left one another and gone different ways.

A moment later the door was quietly opened, a white face looked out, and a hand waved them in. Very quietly the three went through the door and it was at once locked behind them. They followed the man along one garden path after another until they came to the kitchen door of the house. A candle was burning in the large empty kitchen. The man who led them took it up and went before them up a great many stairs, turning every now and again to make sure that they made as little noise as possible. Colonel Geraldine went after him, the box of swords under one arm and a pistol ready in the other hand. Brackenbury's heart beat quickly. If he had not faced danger all his life, this dark place would have frightened him very much.

At the top of the stairs the man with the candle threw open a door and led the three officers into a small room lit by a smoky lamp. Beside the fire sat a fine-looking man of middle age.

"Welcome," said he, as he held out a hand to Colonel Geraldine. "I knew I could count on your doing as I asked."

"You can count on my whole life, sir," said the Colonel with a bow.

"Who are your friends?" asked the first man, and Geraldine told him their names. The other man made them welcome.

"It is good of you to come, gentlemen," he said. "This will not be a pleasant night, I warn you. But men like you are always quick to help in time of danger."

"Your Highness," said the Major, "I cannot hide what I know. You cannot be Mr Godall. You are Prince Florizel of Bohemia!"

Florizel bowed. "I am sometimes known by the other name," he said. "You would both have served Mr Godall, I am sure, but the Prince, perhaps, may do more for you. I am happy to have you with me tonight."

They talked together for a time and then the strange man who had brought them into the house came forward with his watch in his hand and whispered in the Prince's ear.

"I am ready, Dr Noel," answered Florizel aloud. He turned to the others. "Now, gentlemen, I must leave you in darkness. The time has come."

The man called Dr Noel put out the lamp. Through the window they could see the pale grey sky of early morning, but it was not enough to give light in the room. When the Prince rose to his feet no one could see his face. He went to the door and waited there, just inside the room, then spoke in a low voice.

"Please keep very quiet," he said. "Do not talk or move about. Hide yourselves in the shadows."

For nearly ten minutes the only sound in Rochester House was made by the rats that ran about behind the old walls. Then a step was heard on the stair, coming nearer and nearer, very slowly and carefully, as if the man were listening all the time for danger. A hand touched the door and it opened slowly, letting in a little more of the morning light. The figure of a man stood there, silent, without moving. Even in the dim light they could see his mouth open like a dog that had been hunted, and his teeth shining. One thing was plain. He had been over the head in water only a minute or two before. While he stood there the drops fell from his wet clothes and made a dripping sound on the floor.

The next moment he came in, and all of a sudden the Prince leapt forward. There was a cry and a wild struggle. Before Colonel Geraldine could come to his help the Prince held the man in his strong arms.

"Dr Noel," he said, "will you please re-light the lamp."

When there was light he told Geraldine and Brackenbury to hold his prisoner and walked over to the other side of the room. Prince Florizel of Bohemia now stood facing the President of the Suicide Club once again.

"President," he said, "you laid a trap for me, but your

own feet are caught in it. The day is beginning—it is your last morning. You have swum across the Regent's Canal to come here secretly. It is the last water you will bathe in. Your old friend Dr Noel who helped you to dig the grave in the garden has given you into my hands. You have no friends now in the whole world. That grave you dug for me will hold you. Kneel down and pray, sir, if you wish, for your time is short. God and man are tired of your wicked ways."

The President spoke no word and made no sign, but hung his head and kept his eyes on the floor.

"Gentlemen," the Prince went on, "this man escaped me for a long time. His life has been full of evil. Now we must duel to the death, for I have made up my mind that he is to die."

Colonel Geraldine opened the box of swords.

"Quick, sir," said the Prince to the President, "choose a sword and do not keep me waiting. I wish to be done with you for ever."

For the first time the President raised his head.

"Is it to be between you and me?" he asked eagerly.

"That is the chance I am giving you," answered the Prince. "I cannot put you to death by murder, and I gave you my word that I would not tell the world about the Suicide Club. It must be by fair fight, a duel between the two of us."

"Well then," cried the President, "who knows what may happen? I may win yet, and if not, I shall die at the hand of one of the finest gentlemen in Europe."

The Colonel and the Lieutenant took away their hands, and the President went to the table where the box of swords lay and chose one with great care. He smiled now, as if he were sure of winning the fight. The others began to be afraid, and begged Prince Florizel to change his mind.

"He is only playing a game," he said. "I think I can promise you gentlemen that it will not be for long."

"Your Highness must be careful," said Colonel Geraldine.

"Geraldine," said the Prince, "did you ever know me fail when my mind was made up? I owe you this man's death for your brother's sake, and you shall have it."

The President lifted a sword and said he was ready. The Prince took one also, almost without looking at it.

"Colonel Geraldine and Dr Noel," he said, "you will please wait in this room. Major O'Rooke, you are an older man, and know all about a duel. Will you go with the President? Lieutenant Rich, please be good enough to come with me."

"Your Highness," answered Brackenbury, "I am happy to be at your side."

"Then let us go," said Prince Florizel, and led the way out of the room and down the stairs.

The two men who were left in the room opened the window to try to hear what was happening in the garden below. The rain was now over, day had almost come, and the birds were singing their morning song in every tree and bush. The Prince and the others had gone from sight and sound.

"He has taken him down beside the grave," said Dr Noel.

"God!" cried the Colonel. "God save the right!"

They waited in silence. Many minutes passed, the day grew brighter, and the birds still sang their happy song. Then came the sound of footsteps on the stairs. It was the Prince and the two officers who came in. God had saved the right.

"Look, Geraldine," said the Prince, throwing his sword on the floor. "There is the blood of the man who killed your brother. Think of the many he has hurt or sent to their death! What evil he has done! Now all that is finished for ever. Let us never again speak of the Suicide Club and its wicked President."